HARVEST HOUSE PUBLISHERS
Eugene, Oregon 97402

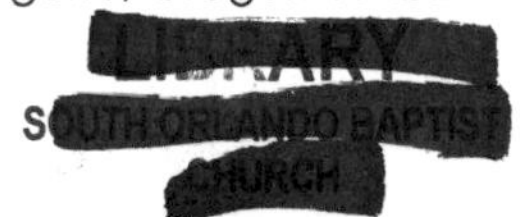

MRS. JULIA THOMPSEN

MR. JOHN McABE THOMPSEN

KATIE THOMPSEN

BETH McKINNEY

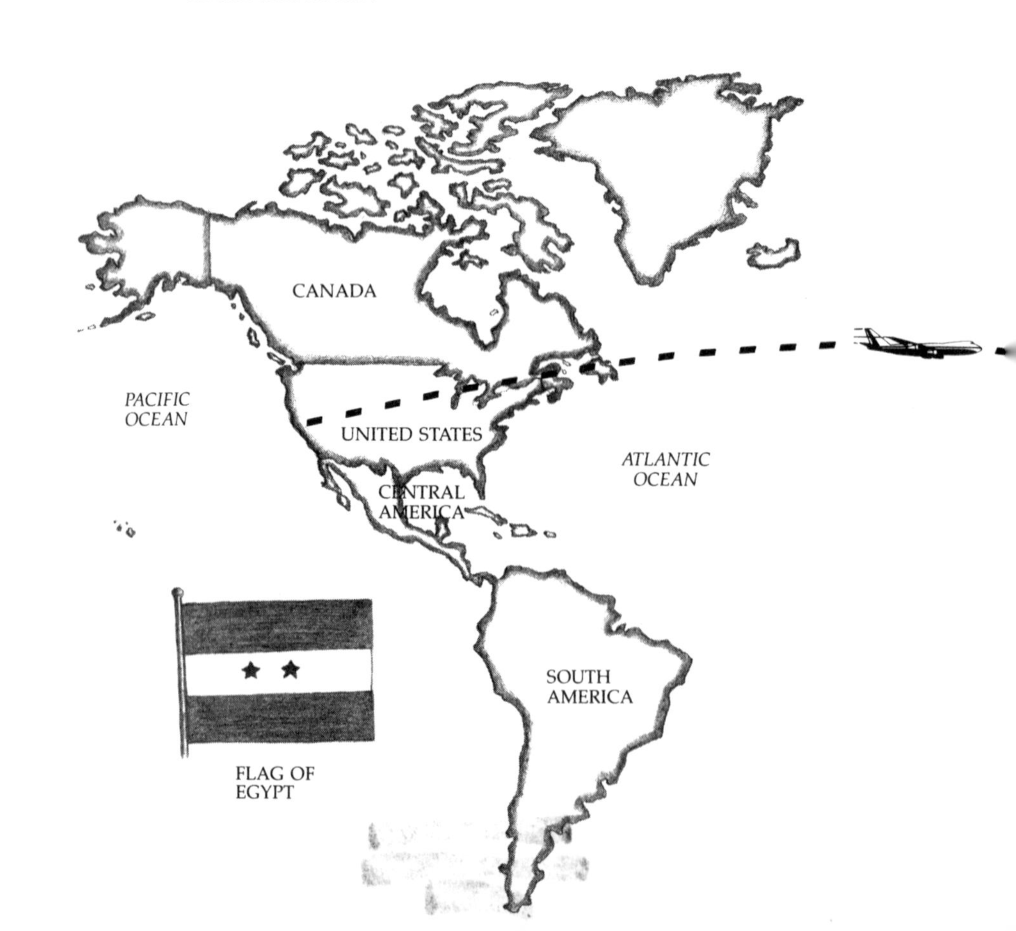

PETER THOMPSEN

HAMID REZA

MOHAMMED

KATIE SAILS THE NILE

Library of Congress Cataloging-in-Publication Data

Mezek, Karen, 1956-
Katie sails the Nile / Karen Mezek.
Summary: A mysterious letter from an old friend of her father's brings Katie and her brother Pete to Egypt, where they encounter a conspiracy involving theft and terrorism.
ISBN 0-89081-814-2
[1. Egypt—Fiction. 2. Mystery and detective stories.]
I. Title.
PZ7.M5748Kat 1990
[Fic]—dc20 90-33471
CIP
AC

Printed in the United States of America.

Katie
Sails the Nile

Chapter 1

A Cry for Help!

"Breakfast, Katie! Hurry up or you'll be late for school!"

Katie threw her schoolbag over her shoulder and raced down the stairs. Careening around the corner, she dropped her bag in the kitchen doorway and grabbed a bowl of oatmeal from her mother's outstretched hand.

"Sit down at the table, Katie," her mother insisted. "And move your books out of the doorway. Someone may trip—"

"Yeoow!" cried her brother Peter as he came dashing around the corner, running smack into Katie's schoolbag.

"Ooops," said Katie. "Sorry, Pete."

"A deliberate booby trap," her brother grumbled.

Katie's father, Mr. John McAbe Thompsen, was sitting at the table drinking his coffee and watching the commotion with his usual calm. "Come on, you two, sit down and eat your breakfast." He waited until both children were seated, then bowed his head and prayed, "Dear Lord, thank you for this food and for a brand new day. Bless each one of us at school and at work. Amen."

"It's *supposed* to be a brand new day," complained Katie as she started to eat, "but sometimes I feel like every day is exactly the same. I need some excitement in my life!"

"You know what would be exciting?" said Mrs. Thompsen. "If you got an 'A' on your math test today."

Katie winced. "Math—ugh!"

Just then the doorbell rang. "Answer that, will you Katie?" asked her mother.

Katie groaned and got up from the table. When she opened the door, she saw a frail young man with black hair and nervous eyes. He wore a tattered jacket, and the old tennis shoes on his feet had holes in the toes.

"Is this the home of Mr. John McAbe Thompsen?" he asked in a strong foreign accent.

Before Katie could say "Yes," the man had thrust a crumpled envelope into her hand. "Give this letter to him," he said. "It is urgent!"

Katie glanced down at the envelope and back up again. Already, the man was scurrying down the street as fast as his thin little legs could carry him.

"Weird. *Very* weird," thought Katie as she walked slowly back to the kitchen. Examining the envelope, she noticed it was blank except for some writing in one corner. "Why, that's in Arabic . . . I *think*," she said in surprise.

Handing the letter to her father, Katie quickly told him what had happened. She noticed a growing look of concern as he read the mysterious message.

"This is just about the strangest letter I've ever received. I'm not quite sure what to make of it—except that the man who wrote it seems to be asking for my help," he said as he looked up.

"Who? Who's asking for help?" Katie asked eagerly.

"Yeah," said Peter. "What's it about?"

"No time for explanations," their mother announced. "It's off to school with you two—right this minute!"

"Oh, please tell us!" they pleaded.

"Not now," said their father. "Perhaps when you get home." Again he was eyeing the letter in his hand with a troubled frown.

All day long, Katie had a tough time concentrating on her schoolwork. She kept thinking about the letter and its mysterious contents. When it came time for the math test, she tried hard to put the events of the morning out of her mind and do her very best. As she wrote her final answer she screwed her eyes shut and said, "Please, Lord, an 'A' this time."

At lunch Katie hurried to find a place to sit with her best friend Beth. "Let's not sit with anyone else today," she whispered breathlessly. "I've got something 'top secret' to tell you."

When the story had been told, Beth nodded, "Well, it *does* sound interesting. But that doesn't necessarily mean it's top secret," she added.

"Of course it is!" cried Katie. "How often do people get letters with Arabic writing on them, delivered by frightened little men in old jackets and beat-up tennis shoes? That letter's got something important inside—why, it's a cry for help!" she finished dramatically.

"Okay, okay, don't get so excited! But it seems to me that since your father is a news reporter—"

"He's a foreign correspondent," Katie corrected her.

"Yes, he's a *foreign*-whatever. And that means he must get letters from all over the place." Beth chewed on a carrot stick thoughtfully. "Although I *do* admit that was a pretty strange way to deliver a letter."

Katie nodded her head fervently. "You bet it was! Now Beth, I know there have been times when I've let my imagination run away with me. And I admit that it's gotten me into trouble more than once. But not this time! This letter means something special—it means excitement!!"

Chapter 2

Secret Passwords

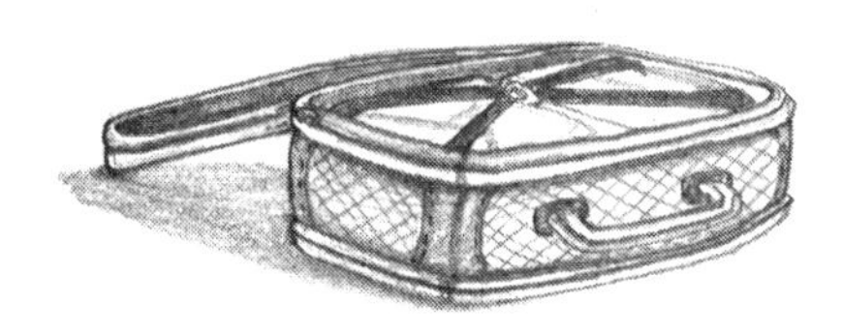

That afternoon, as usual, Katie, Beth and Peter all walked home from school together.

"Just think," Beth said joyously. "Easter vacation starts in two days!"

"And what better way to begin a holiday than with a mystery!" cried Katie, skipping down the sidewalk and swinging her schoolbag.

"Shh!—don't talk so loud," said Peter. "There might be spies around. And you shouldn't have told Beth—*she* might be one!" He looked at Katie's friend suspiciously.

Beth narrowed her eyes and put on a wicked grin. "How did you guess? Now that you know I'm a spy, I have no choice but to do away with you!" She threw out her arms and jumped at Peter. Giving a loud shriek, he dashed off down the street.

"Race you home!" he yelled, and disappeared around the corner.

But Katie and Beth were much more interested in talking than in racing.

"Listen," said Katie. "When I find out all about the letter I'll call you. But I won't tell you about it on the phone because it might be bugged. Let's see . . . I'll use a secret password. I'll say 'Easter Parade!'—that's how you'll know it's me on the phone—and then we can meet at my special place up on the hill by the oak tree, okay? We'll be safe there and I can tell you everything."

"Bugged telephones, passwords, secret meetings?" Beth couldn't believe her ears. "Aren't you going a bit too far?"

"Nope," said Katie, running up the driveway to her house. "I'll call you later!"

Hurrying inside, Katie made a beeline for her father's study. She knew he would be there, working on his latest newspaper article. Katie loved to visit her father in his study. The shelves were lined with books, and two huge, over-stuffed chairs sat facing the brick fireplace. In the winter a fire was usually burning, making the room warm and cozy. Now that it was spring, the long French windows were wide open to let in the scent of gardenias.

Mr. Thompsen sat in his old leather chair with his computer lit up in front of him. He was listening to Peter throw questions at him faster than he could answer them.

"Now just hang on," said Mr. Thompsen, laughing and holding up his hands for quiet. "Why don't the two of you sit down and I'll tell you as much as I can."

Without another word, Katie and Peter plopped down on the sofa and looked up expectantly.

Taking off his glasses, Mr. Thompsen smoothed his hair back from his forehead. Although he didn't have as much hair as he used to, the long, mousey brown strands still managed to get in his way. He took a deep breath and began, "The letter was written to me by a man

named Hamid Reza. He lives in Cairo, Egypt, and I met him long ago, before either of you were born. I'm not going to tell you much more about it, because I don't know much myself—except that Hamid's son is in some kind of trouble and he has asked for my help. I'll find out more when I get there."

Katie gasped. "You mean you're going to Egypt—just like that?"

Her father smiled and snapped his fingers. "Yes—just like that!" he said.

"What about *us*?" asked Peter. "Mom's going to take care of Great-Aunt Clara over Easter vacation. Who's going to take care of *us*?"

Their mother's face, framed by dark hair and brightened by smiling eyes, appeared in the study door. "That's what we've been discussing," she told them.

"Oh no!" Katie groaned. "We're not going with you to Great-Aunt Clara's, are we?" Her great-aunt was a feisty, fiery-tempered old lady who wasn't at all fond of children. She'd never had any of her own and had no patience with such a lively pair as they.

"No, don't worry. I think we can find something better than that for you to do," her father replied. "How would you two like to spend your holiday with me in Egypt?"

Two excited whoops echoed in unison. "Just wait 'til I tell Beth!" Katie cried, jumping out of her seat.

"Wait a minute, young lady," said Mr. Thompsen, putting an arm on her shoulder before she could fly out of the room. "We haven't much time to get ready—only two days—so I expect both of you to help as much as possible."

"Oh, yes," Katie and Peter promised enthusiastically. "But can I just call Beth and tell her?" Katie pleaded.

Peter looked horrified. "Don't let her! Beth could be a spy!"

"Honestly, Pete," cried his mother. "Where do you get such ideas? Katie, go on and call Beth and then do your homework. My goodness, but we have a lot to do!"

Impatiently, Katie dialed Beth's number.

"Hello?" Beth answered.

"Easter Parade!" Katie gasped breathlessly.

"What? Oh, yes—Easter Parade. Why do you have to say that? I know it's you!"

"Shh! Listen, I've got the most *incredible* news for you!" Katie whispered into the telephone.

"And why are you whispering? The telephone is *not* bugged, you know. And even if it was, they can still hear you if you whisper!"

"Beth!" Katie wailed. "Sometimes I wonder how we *ever* got to be best friends! If you'd just listen for a minute! I have to do my homework now, but I'll meet you at the special place at 5 o'clock. Got that?"

"Okay," said Beth. "But I wish you'd just tell me. I'm dying to know!"

"At 5 o'clock," Katie repeated. "Easter Parade, over and out."

"Easter Parade, over and out," Beth answered reluctantly.

At 5 o'clock on the dot, a small figure could be seen on the hill behind the Thompsen house, pacing back and forth beneath the oak tree.

"Oh, where is she?" Katie wondered. In a few minutes she'd have to go home for supper.

Beth's curly brown head appeared over the side of the hill and Katie ran eagerly to meet her.

"This better be worth it," Beth huffed, looking up at the cloudy sky. "I think it's going to rain any minute."

"Oh, who cares about that," said Katie. She took a deep breath. "Beth, I'm going to Eygpt!"

Beth's jaw dropped open. "You're not!"

"I am! Dad's going to take me and Pete. That letter was from a friend of his, asking for help. We leave the day after tomorrow!"

"Katie! That's not fair—I want to go too!"

Katie suddenly looked crestfallen. "I wish you could come. We went to Switzerland together and had such a wonderful time—remember?"

Beth nodded her head. "You're going to go off and have great adventures, and I won't be there to make sure you stay out of trouble!"

Katie gave her friend a big hug. "I don't know how I'll ever survive without you, but I'll try. And I promise to write everything down in my diary and read it to you when I get back. That way you can imagine you were there with me."

"I guess that will have to do," said Beth, sounding depressed. Then she smiled bravely. "I'm happy for you, really I am. Just write it all down like you promised. I'll be thinking of you every minute!"

After agreeing that Beth should come over the next afternoon to help Katie pack, they said good-bye. Katie began running down the hill, her straight brown hair flying in the wind. "Oh wow—excitement, adventure," she panted. "Did I say I was *bored*?!"

Suddenly she stopped for a moment, glancing back up toward the solitary oak tree—*her* tree—as it stood carved against the sky. Soon she'd be in Egypt, in an exotic world of intrigue, romance and danger. Katie felt sure she would be a different person when she returned, and she hoped the change would be for the better. It was reassuring to know the tree would stay the same. Patiently it would wait for her, standing still and silent under sun and moon . . . day after unchanging day.

I'll be back soon, Katie whispered to the tree, and *I'll tell you everything!*

Chapter 3

Dust and Heat

The next two days raced by in a whirlwind of activity. With each passing moment, Mrs. Thompsen became more and more worried and seemed to be regretting her decision to let Katie and Peter go.

"I can't believe I agreed to let you all run off like this!" she said when the time came to say good-bye, giving each of them a kiss. "Call me the minute you arrive!" she told her husband.

Turning to the children, she offered one last word of advice. "I know you think of this as a big adventure, but you might find when you get to Egypt that it isn't as romantic or exciting as you dreamed it would be. It's a poor country and life is much harder there than it is here. You'll probably see some unpleasant, perhaps even shocking things. I'll look forward to talking to you about your experiences when you return. I love you and I'll be praying for you!"

Just as Katie was stepping into the car, she heard Beth's voice calling from down the street.

"Wait a sec! Don't go yet." Beth ran up to Katie and flung her arms around her. "Have a great trip," she said, pushing a little package into Katie's hand. "It's something useful," she explained.

"Thanks!" yelled Katie as the car drove off. "I'll see you soon!"

In the airport waiting room, Katie opened Beth's present. It was a beautiful little pen, decorated with pink and purple glitter.

"For your diary. To make sure you write your very best!" said the note attached to it. Katie smiled. Beth was the greatest!

Soon the Thompsens were leaving their California home far behind, soaring high above the earth. Across the United States they flew, with a brief stop in New York, then on to Cairo, Egypt. Katie managed to sleep for most of the trip, feeling quite refreshed when they arrived late that evening.

The moment they walked out of the airport

the Thompsens were greeted by a blast of dry heat and a hoard of eager taxi drivers, pushing and shoving each other and all crying at once, "'Scuse me, 'scuse me!" "Pleeze, this way!" "Special deal, just for you!"

One stubborn little man managed to squeeze his way to the front. He was dressed in a long, cream colored robe. A battered fez—a red cone-shaped hat with a black tassel—was perched on his head.

"Is he wearing a nightgown?" Peter whispered loudly into Katie's ear.

"No, silly," she whispered back. "That's how they dress here."

"'Scuse me," said the little man, giving a slight bow. "I take you to hotel right by pyramids. Someone waiting there to see you. You understand, yes, yes?"

Mr. Thompsen eyed the man sharply. "Okay," he said, motioning Katie and Peter to follow.

They climbed into a dusty old car that looked as if it would fall apart any minute. There followed one of the most frightening experiences of Katie's entire life—a ride through the streets of Cairo. Neither drivers nor pedestrians seemed to follow any rules. Horns blared nonstop,

donkeys brayed, people shouted, buses belched out fumes, and brakes never stopped screeching.

Katie was sure she was going to die when two cars, coming from opposite directions, almost slammed into them. She had hardly recovered from that close call when a donkey stuck its head right in her window and brayed into her ear. Her heart froze, and her ears rang painfully.

All the while, their driver never stopped talking. Sometimes he even took his hands off the steering wheel and waved them in the air to make his point. Repeatedly Mr. Thompsen lunged at the controls and then nervously dropped his hands into his lap.

"Such a great honor to meet you, Mr. John Thompsen!" the man said. "I must introduce myself. I am Abdul." He beamed proudly, revealing two gold front teeth. Turning away from the steering wheel, he began shaking hands with each of them.

"Yikes!" cried Peter, sinking into his seat and covering his eyes. "I think I'm going to be sick!" There was a loud screech of brakes as Abdul missed the car in front of them by a hair.

Abdul immediately leapt out of the car, shaking his fists and yelling at the top of his voice. After a few moments he got back inside, smiled happily at his passengers, and drove on.

"Am I to understand you are a friend of Hamid Reza?" Mr. Thompsen asked.

"A friend, yes, and I am also his brother!" Abdul laughed loudly, as if he had told a funny joke. "Ahh! But does he have a story for you! You must listen to him and then put it in newspapers. Oh, yes, yes! You will see!" He nodded his head wildly and the children watched in fascination as his hat teetered from side to side.

Eventually the crowds and the noisy streets gave way to the quieter outskirts of the city. But one thing did not change—the dust. It was everywhere. A thick layer covered the old squashed-together buildings, the roads, the inside of the car. Katie felt it on her clothes and behind her neck. Dust, heat and the smell of sweat! It made Katie ill. How she longed for a cool shower and a clean bed!

She soon forgot her discomfort however, when their driver suddenly informed them, "Look! The Nile River—and also the pyramids!" Beyond the dark, immense waters of the Nile three sharp points rose before them, dramatically lit and standing against a backdrop of clear night sky and shimmering stars.

"Oh!" breathed Katie.

"Wow!" echoed Peter.

Never before, and never since, would Katie have such a feeling of mystery and awe. The old car rumbled on noisily as Katie and Peter gazed out the window at the approaching shapes. They had been built thousands of years ago as burial places for some of Egypt's ancient rulers.

"You can visit pyramids tomorrow," said Abdul. "But for now—here we are at hotel!"

The car jolted to a stop and the Thompsens tumbled out gratefully.

"Thank goodness we're still alive," Peter whispered to his sister.

"I have rooms all arranged. One for young lady," Abdul bowed and doffed his hat. "And one for gentlemen."

Suddenly, Katie felt very tired. She was relieved when a bellboy took their suitcases and led them up the stairs.

She perked up a bit when she saw her room. It was big and airy with a Persian carpet on the floor and an enormous bed. The long windows opened onto a balcony and a refreshing breeze gently blew the thin white curtains. Her sense of adventure returned when she stepped onto the balcony and saw she had a clear view of the pyramids in the distance.

"Oh, this is perfect," Katie sighed. "Absolutely perfect."

"Don't drink the water from the faucet. And make sure you close the mosquito nets *all the way* around your bed or you'll be eaten alive," her father reminded her.

"We're in the room next door if you need anything," he added. "Tomorrow we get up early. Hamid is meeting us for breakfast."

Shutting her door, Katie peeled off her sweaty clothes and got into the shower. How wonderful it felt to wash away the dirt and grime! Then she climbed into bed, carefully pulling the mosquito nets all around her. Sticking her arm through the netting, she turned off the light and closed her eyes.

I promised Beth I'd write everything in my diary, she thought sleepily. *But I'll just have to do it in the morning . . . I'm so-oo tired . . .*

How she wished Beth were here! Traveling just wasn't the same without her best friend.

Chapter 4

Mysterious Mr. Reza

The next morning the Thompsens were down to breakfast by 7 o'clock. At last Katie and Peter were going to meet the mysterious Hamid Reza!

Mr. Thompsen noticed Hamid coming across the room and got up to greet him. Katie and Peter saw a very round old man with sparkling white teeth and a fuzzy beard. The neat black suit he was wearing clashed oddly with the sandals on his feet and the turban on his head. His face wore a worried look.

"My good friend," he said in a low voice, shaking Mr. Thompsen's hand. "How happy I am to see you once again. And to meet your two fine children."

Mr. Reza sat down and ordered mint tea. "Uh, John McAbe, my apologies, but I, ahem, had expected to speak to you alone." He glanced at Katie and Peter and stopped, embarrassed.

"Oh, feel free to talk in front of them—they're my assistants," Mr. Thompsen assured him.

Katie and Peter smiled proudly. Eager to hear what Mr. Reza had to say, they leaned forward expectantly.

With a quick glance around the room, Hamid began his story. "As you know, John, I have a shop in the city. I do quite a good business, buying and selling antiques and art treasures. Recently, I discovered some pieces were missing—the most valuable being a dagger inlaid with priceless jewels. It was used in ancient times for religious purposes," he explained to the children. "The worst of it is that I have since found out that it was my own son, Ali, who stole these items—right from under my nose! Ten days ago he disappeared!"

"Did you go to the police?" asked Mr. Thompsen.

Mr. Reza looked alarmed. "No!" he almost shrieked. He clapped a hand over his mouth, horrified at his outburst. Mopping his forehead nervously with a delicate hanky, he continued. "It is all so complicated," he moaned.

Lowering his voice even further, Hamid explained, "My son was forced by a group of terrorists to steal these treasures. They will sell the antiques and use the money to buy weapons to kill people! When I discovered the thefts and asked my son, he confessed to me." Mr. Hamid's voice broke and he wiped his eyes. "They have kidnapped my son. If I tell the police, I will never see him again!"

"Unreal!" breathed Peter.

Mr. Thompsen gave him a stern look and motioned for quiet.

"Will you help me?" Mr. Reza pleaded, his large eyes filled with fear.

"Of course," Mr. Thompsen promised. "I'll do what I can, although I'm not quite sure how I can help you."

"Believe me, there is a reason why I have turned to you. The leader of the terrorist group, Achmed, knows and respects you. Perhaps if you speak to him, he will release my son. If not, we are both lost!" He leaned forward and whispered carefully, "But listen my friends! Allow me to introduce a plan. Achmed has agreed to meet you, but only under the greatest secrecy. Tonight we must travel to the old city of Luxor, in the south. We will sail on my nephew's boat—up the Nile River."

Mr. Thompsen thought carefully for a moment. "We'll accompany you to Luxor, Hamid. But we must discuss this more thoroughly on the boat to be sure there is no danger—especially for my children."

Hamid rose and shook hands gratefully. "I must go now. Thank you so much! We will meet tonight at 10 o'clock by the docks. Abdul will show you the way."

"Well," said Mr. Thompsen after Mr. Reza had gone, "this is certainly turning into more than I bargained for!"

"Wait 'til Beth hears about this! Sailing down the Nile River. I can't believe it!" Katie exclaimed.

"*Up* the Nile River, not down," Mr. Thompsen corrected her. "Well, we still have the whole day in front of us. How about a trip to the pyramids?"

The taxi ride was a blur of humanity, animals and vehicles, all fighting for space on the crowded roadway. Camels and donkeys outnumbered cars on the road. Arabs cycled by in flowing robes, balancing huge trays of freshly baked bread on their heads. Trucks roared past, coughing black fumes. Donkeys and camels ambled along oblivious to the honking horns and screeching brakes.

Finally, the Thompsens' taxi stopped beside a cluster of camels and eager guides. Mr. Thompsen chose one of the guides and discovered that a camel ride to the entrance of the pyramids was included in the tour. Mounted at last on the huge beasts, and giggling nervously, the three set out for the stone structures rising from the hot desert floor.

Their guide, a sturdy old man with a wealth of information, had lived under the shadow of the pyramids for 23 years. "I am the all-time champion pyramid climber—five minutes up and

two minutes down," he told them proudly.

Katie felt goosebumps on her neck as she entered the massive tomb of one of Egypt's ancient kings. It was a steep climb up a dark, narrow passageway to the small chamber where the coffin was housed.

"This tomb took 30 years to build," their guide told them. "It was made especially for the body of the pharaoh. The ancient Egyptians believed the pharaoh was a god and that he would live in his tomb and travel to another world after death. But the only way he could do that was if he was preserved, or mummified."

"I know all about that," said Peter importantly. "They had to take all his insides out and put them in jars. Then they wrapped the body in cloth and put it in a coffin."

"That's disgusting," said Katie. "Just the sort of thing you *would* know!"

"Very good," the guide told Peter. "It was important to the people that the pharaoh be preserved. Because he was their god, they had no life without him. If he was assured entrance into the afterlife, then even the poorest peasant was assured of it also. Better than your Christian religion, isn't it?" he added with a twinkle.

Mr. Thompsen smiled. "Not really. As Christians, each one of us can come directly to God. We don't depend on another person for our salvation."

Katie walked around the tiny room, breathing in the cool air. She tried to imagine what it must have looked like before the grave robbers came and stole everything. It was empty now of all but the bare stone coffin.

When they returned to the hotel, Katie packed up her few belongings in preparation for their journey up the Nile. The rest of the day was spent wandering through the crowded and noisy bazaars. Both Katie and Peter gingerly tried their first sips of mint tea and were surprised by the pleasant taste. The cool, refreshing drink seemed to be the only way to satisfy their never-ending thirst.

As the flaming red sun set behind the desert hills, Katie felt her excitement growing. And when the ghostly figure of Abdul appeared from out of the shadows and whispered, "It is time. Follow me," her heart beat wildly.

Whatever will happen next? she thought. There was only one way to find out. Picking up her small suitcase firmly in one hand, she stepped out into the darkness.

Chapter 5

Up The Nile

"Am I dreaming?" Katie wondered as Abdul's battered car rumbled along the bumpy road. She decided she wasn't, when a particularly large bump lifted her off her seat and smacked her head against the window. "Ouch!" she cried.

The headlights made only a slight dent in the darkness. Every once in a while a robed figure or a donkey or camel would suddenly appear in front of them, only to be swallowed again by the night as the car passed by.

Making a sudden turn, they stopped. Abdul got out his flashlight and led them to the boat. Katie walked up a narrow plank, holding tightly onto her father's hand. Then he went back to help Peter. The night behind the tiny lantern's ray was pitch black.

Stepping into the light, the face of Hamid Reza suddenly appeared. "Allow me to introduce my nephew, Mohammed. He will sail the boat," Mr. Reza told them. Dimly, Katie made out the face of a teenage boy.

Why he's hardly taller than I am! she thought in surprise. *I bet he's about 16 or 17 years old!*

Mohammed led the Thompsens down to a tiny sleeping cabin. Etched in the darkness was a bunk bed built into the wall. "For Peter and Katie," Mohammed said carefully, trying to pronounce their names perfectly in English. Beyond was another tiny cabin for their father and Hamid Reza.

"Thanks," said Katie and Peter, smiling. It was hard to tell in the darkness whether or not he smiled back.

"I want the top bunk," Peter immediately announced when they were alone, and climbed up.

"I *knew* you'd say that!" Katie said, sorry she hadn't been quicker. "Oh, take it if you want!—but I get it tomorrow night!"

"Hmmmn," Peter mumbled, his face buried in the pillow.

As Katie got into bed the boat groaned and began to move. They were casting off. All night long, while they slept, the Nile would flow beneath them.

In the morning I'll find myself in the middle of the Nile River! Katie thought wonderingly. *I hope I don't get seasick!*

"Good-night Pete," she said softly. But the only answer she got was his soft, steady breathing.

The next morning Katie woke up early. Curious as she was to go up on deck, she made herself open her diary and write everything that had happened the day before. By the time she had finished, Peter was awake as well and they went upstairs together.

"Hello there!" called Mohammed, standing at the helm of the boat. "Did you sleep well?"

"Oh yes, thank you," replied Katie, feeling suddenly shy.

Mohammed loved his boat dearly and sailed it with affection and assurance. Sometimes, grasping his long robe between his teeth so he could move easier, he would adjust a sail or pull on one of the ropes. He looked so confident and graceful.

While Peter talked with Mohammed about his boat, Katie sat down on the deck and looked

straight up at the sky. She imagined herself in the middle of a giant bowl. Moving her head slowly around, she followed the enormous deep blue arc until it met the brown earth in the distance. Along the river-front, the earth turned green. Her eyes followed the green down to the water's edge and all the way across to the other side of the Nile. Then she followed the arc back again until she was once more looking straight up at the sky.

"Do you spend a lot of time sailing your boat?" Katie asked Mohammed.

"Oh yes," he answered. "It is my job, you know. I take many tourists. When I am not sailing, I live in a village by the river—just like that one," he pointed to a ramshackle bunch of mud huts on the bank.

Before long they were discussing Mohammed's uncle and the terrible trouble he was in. "Do you think he will ever get the dagger again?" Peter asked. "Perhaps his son could steal it back when my dad helps him get away."

Mohammed looked puzzled. "I am sorry, perhaps I did not understand. I know many things were stolen, but I did not hear of this dagger. I did not realize my uncle had anything as valuable as that in his shop."

"Of course," Katie told him. "He has lots of valuable things—and the dagger was priceless!"

Mohammed shook his head, thinking hard. "I know he used to have many expensive treasures, but I thought that was long ago. I have never heard of this dagger." He shrugged his shoulders. "But perhaps I am mistaken. I am not an expert in these things and I could be wrong."

"Well, good morning!" a voice boomed behind them. It was Hamid Reza climbing onto the deck. He looked nervous and unhappy. "I do not like boats," he complained, gripping the rail and walking gingerly along the deck.

Peter leaned over to his sister and whispered, "I always thought there was something fishy about this whole business. I don't trust that Mr. Reza!"

"Don't be silly," she whispered back. "Mohammed doesn't know everything. It wouldn't make sense if Mr. Reza wasn't telling the truth. What would be the point?"

"Time for breakfast," Mohammed announced cheerfully. "My, but sailing does give one an appetite!"

Mr. Reza groaned and sat down. Getting out his handkerchief, he wiped his brow with a shaky hand. "If it were not for the sake of my son, I would not stay on this contraption a moment longer!"

Fortunately, no one else seemed bothered by sailing. Katie found she had a terrific appetite and had no trouble eating two hard boiled eggs and three pieces of flat pita bread spread with tomatoes and cheese.

After breakfast, Mr. Reza and Mr. Thompsen huddled together in a corner and discussed their plans for freeing Ali. Later on in the afternoon Katie and Peter managed to get their father alone, and told him about their conversation with Mohammed.

"So you see," Katie finished, "it's just possible that Mr. Reza is lying about the dagger being stolen. But if he is, why?"

Mr. Thompsen frowned. "I don't know. But I will certainly try to find out. Perhaps Mohammed is mistaken. He did say he could be wrong. In any case, this is something for *me* to investigate. The two of you are just along for the ride, remember that," he told them sternly.

The rest of the journey passed pleasantly enough, with Katie and Peter eager to learn all about sailing and Mohammed happy to teach them. When the boat finally docked outside Luxor three days later, they were sorry to say good-bye to their new friend.

Mohammed bowed to them both and to their father. "It has been my greatest pleasure to accompany you. I hope the rest of your trip will be successful."

As Katie was about to step off the boat Mohammed called to her. "Wait one moment," he said. "I would only like to say, my uncle is a good man and I have no doubt that he is in great trouble. I am sure I must have made a mistake about the dagger, since I really do not know about such things. I am sorry if I caused you to be concerned."

"Don't worry," she told him. "If anything strange is going on, my dad will find out about it. Thanks so much for everything—especially for teaching us how to sail!" she called as she jumped off the end of the wooden plank.

Their hotel was not far from the shore, and Mr. Reza quickly led them to the entrance. He seemed more nervous than ever and his breath came in short, rasping gulps. "I leave you here," he said. "Tomorrow morning I take you, John, to see Achmed. This is a secret meeting and *no one* must know about it. The children, of course, will stay here."

Katie and Peter were about to protest, but a look from their father told them it would be useless. Defeated, they climbed up the stairs to their separate rooms.

Katie's room wasn't nearly as nice as in the last hotel. The water that came out of the tap had a brown tint to it and the bathroom looked slightly dirty. Worst of all, there was no mosquito net around the bed.

Buzzz—buuzzz . . . came a sound in her ear that evening as she lay down. Katie swatted the air and shook her head furiously, but the sound came back. Too hot to retreat under the covers, the entire night was spent between fitful sleep and wild slaps. At one point, ready for battle, Katie got out of bed, turned on the light and began swatting mosquitoes when they landed on the walls. But for every insect she killed, two more took its place.

Admitting defeat at last, Katie got back into bed, leaving the walls covered with red and black smears. Only by dawn did she fall into a deep sleep. She awoke later to find herself covered with tiny red, itchy bumps. At breakfast, Katie saw that her father and Peter hadn't fared any better. Peter was scratching frantically and looking miserable.

"Okay, here's the plan," said Mr. Thompsen. "After breakfast, Hamid will pick me up and take me to meet Achmed. And don't worry," he said when he saw their looks of alarm, "I can take care of myself. You two can wander about on your own, but stay near the hotel! The desk clerk said there's a pharmacy just around the corner with medicine for your bites. Here's some money. I suggest you go there first thing."

Katie and Peter reluctantly went off in search of the pharmacy. Outside, they were blasted once again by the now familiar heat and noisy streets. Following the desk clerk's directions, they turned left at the first corner.

"It should be here on the right, just past the cafe," said Katie. She saw tables set up outside under shady trees and little groups of men drinking thick Turkish coffee. Her eyes began to move beyond, looking for the pharmacy, but something brought her gaze back again. Gasping in surprise, she grabbed Peter by the arm.

"There's someone I know!" she cried, staring at two young men huddled at a table in a far corner.

"You must be kidding!" Peter said in disbelief.

"No, I'm sure of it. It's the man who delivered the letter to Dad back home!"

"Well, let's go talk to him," Peter suggested, making his way between the tables.

"Excuse me," said Katie when they were quite close. "Don't I know you—"

The skinny, dark-haired man looked up, startled. His eyes grew round with fear when he recognized Katie. Before she could finish her sentence, he had grabbed the young man next to him and started to run away.

"Let's go," cried Katie as she and Peter dashed after them.

They knew they could never catch the two long-legged runaways, but that didn't stop them from trying. Just as the two men were about to break free of the tables, one of them tripped over a chair and both went sprawling to the ground. Katie and Peter pounced on them and, surprisingly, they didn't try to escape.

"What's the matter?" Katie asked, helping them up. "Why did you run away?"

The skinny little man dusted himself off hurriedly. "Forgive me, please. When I saw you, I was so startled. All I could think of was to get away."

By now, everyone in the cafe was staring at them and the man and his friend motioned for the two children to follow them.

"We can talk here," he said, leading them a short distance down the road. "My name is Ishmael and this is Ali Reza—Hamid Reza's son!"

Katie and Peter stared in frightened disbelief at the man's companion. Certainly, he *looked* like a younger version of Mr. Reza—chubby and with a beard sprouting on his chin.

"I sorry," Hamid Reza's son said miserably. "My father do very bad thing. Mr. Thompsen—great danger!"

Chapter 6

Betrayed!

Katie gulped. What was he saying? Could it be that Hamid Reza had betrayed their father and was at this very moment leading him into a deadly trap?

"We must go to the police!" Katie told them.

"There is no time," answered Ishmael. He hurried off down the street and Katie and Peter raced behind him. "We will take my car and follow them. It is much faster than Hamid's and I know a short-cut. We can reach them before they meet Achmed!"

Once inside the car and on their way, Katie asked for an explanation.

"Ali speaks very poor English so I will speak for him," said Ishmael. "Since I am Ali's best friend, Hamid sent me with the letter for your father. I must tell you that when I delivered it to your house, I truly believed that what it said was true."

Katie gave a horrified gasp. "You mean it wasn't?" She looked from one to the other. "You mean . . . it was a *lie*?"

"Yes," he said, terribly unhappy. "It was a way to get your father to come here. Hamid Reza needs money desperately. His business is not going well and Achmed offered him a large sum of money if he could convince your father to come here. When Achmed meets your father he will take him as a hostage, just as many others have been taken hostage by terrorists in our war-torn part of the world. I did not realize the truth until I came back here—Luxor is my home—and Ali just now got in touch with me. His father sent him on holiday to Switzerland, but he discovered the truth and came to Luxor as quickly as he could."

"I knew it all the time," Peter suddenly announced. "I knew something strange was going on. I never trusted that Reza guy. Remember, I told you so."

"I know," Katie admitted. "And I thought you were wrong."

Once outside the town, it was impossible to talk anymore. The car shook violently as they bounced along at a speed that Katie would not have thought possible under normal circumstances. The road they followed led along the river's edge and on either side were high reeds and bushes. Katie and Peter both screamed as Ishmael suddenly swerved the car right into the center of the brush. On they sped, parting the tall reeds in front of them like a green sea. Holding tightly to each other, they didn't let go until suddenly they emerged into the open again and found themselves once more on the road.

"There's my dad and Mr. Reza," cried Peter, pointing to a car in front of them.

"Yes," said Ishmael, sounding grim. "Thank goodness we caught up with them."

"But what's happening?" Katie asked fearfully. Mr. Reza's car was weaving recklessly from one side of the road to the other.

As Ishmael drove closer, Katie and Peter saw their father and Hamid were wrestling furiously. Abruptly the car swerved off the road and turned over.

Ishmael screeched to a halt and everyone jumped out. With relief, Katie and Peter saw that no one had been hurt. Mr. Thompsen crawled out of the car, dragging Hamid behind him.

"I am innocent," Mr. Reza was yelling at the top of his voice. "I have done nothing wrong, do you hear? Nothing!"

But when he saw his son, his nerve was shattered and he broke down. Crying, he fell to the ground.

"Ahh, what have I done, what have I done?" he cried in anguish. "Forgive me, my son. Forgive me, my friend." Burying his face in his hands, he continued to moan those words over and over.

Gently, Mr. Thompsen reached down and picked him up. "Why have you done this thing?" he asked softly.

Mr. Reza turned his tortured eyes to Mr. Thompsen. "It was for my son," he cried, "for my son! I made bad decisions. I was out of money and my business was in trouble. How could I leave such a disaster for my only child? So I thought of this terrible plan—to betray my friend in order to get a huge sum of money. I convinced myself it was right, but I had no peace. I have been ill since the thought first entered my mind."

Ali hung his head and said nothing. There were tears in his eyes.

"We must go," Mr. Thompsen said. "Any minute the police will be here."

Mr. Reza looked up in terror. "The police?"

"Yes," Mr. Thompsen answered, as he led Hamid towards Ishmael's car. "Thanks to Katie and Peter, I discovered that you weren't being honest with me. You never had a valuable dagger stolen. In fact, you no longer carry valuable objects in your shop. You were too proud to admit your business was failing, and you were greedy, too. You were willing to betray a friend for money."

"It is true," said Mr. Reza, his voice filled with despair.

The ride back to Luxor was uncomfortable, with everyone crowded into Ishmael's tiny car. When they reached the hotel at last, a very dejected Hamid Reza got out and stood before Mr. Thompsen.

"If you called the police, why did we not wait for them to come?" he asked.

Mr. Thompsen looked at Mr. Reza thoughtfully and replied, "I am hoping they have captured Achmed by now, at the place where we were to meet. But you have been my friend in the past, Hamid, and I trust that you are truly sorry for what you have done—not just to me and your son, but also to yourself. I forgive you, and I have decided not to turn you over to the police. That decision I leave up to you."

Mr. Thompsen put an arm around each of his children and led them up the steps of the hotel.

Early the next morning the Thompsens were all packed and ready to leave. Mr. Thompsen had managed, with great difficulty, to call his wife and tell her they were on their way back to Cairo and would soon be coming home.

"I can't go into the details," he said above the crackling static. "But I can tell you this—we will all be happy to come home and see your smiling face!"

At breakfast, Mr. Thompsen bought a copy of the international American newspaper, *The Herald Tribune.* On the front page was a picture of the captured Achmed and a story beneath. But no mention was made of Mr. Thompsen's part in the adventure, or of Hamid Reza's terrible plan.

"I guess Hamid didn't turn himself in," Mr. Thompsen said with disappointment. "Somehow, I felt sure that he would."

"It says here that 'a mysterious phone call tipped them off' and that's how they were able to capture Achmed," said Katie, reading down the page. "Now, who made that mysterious phone call, I wonder?"

Mr. Thompsen pretended innocence and amazement. "I have no idea. Surely you don't think it could have been *me,* do you?"

As they left the hotel, Ali and Ishmael were waiting for them. "We will drive you back to Cairo," Ishmael offered. "It is the least we can do."

"Yes," Ali added, a big smile on his face. "You do good thing for me and my father."

"Well, thank you," said Mr. Thompsen, wondering what on earth could make Ali look so happy. "It will beat having to hire a car."

When they were on their way, Ishmael told them what had happened to Ali's father. "Ali wants you to know that his father turned himself over to the police last night. But he is not in jail! I can only think that because the police were successful and they captured Achmed they are in a very happy mood! When Hamid told them how he had tried to betray you and sell you to Achmed for money, they just laughed and said he must be crazy. So they let him go, even though he tried to insist that they put him in jail!"

Katie and Peter started to laugh. "Wait until I tell Beth this whole, weird story," Katie said. "She'll never believe me!"

"You'd better write it all out very carefully in your diary," her father reminded her. "It's important to get the facts straight while they're still fresh in your mind."

"So where's Mr. Reza now?" Peter asked.

"My father feel bad right now. He not come to say good-bye," Ali answered.

"But he did want us to tell you how thankful he was," Ishmael said. "He realizes now what an evil thing he tried to do. But the fact that you were willing to forgive him has given him hope for the future. He says he knows that God, too, has forgiven him and he will try to start his life afresh."

"Are you going to write an article about this for the newspaper when we get home?" Katie asked her father.

Mr. Thompsen smiled and shook his head. "I think not," he said. "This is one story that is best left untold."

He hugged his daughter affectionately. "However, in your diary you will have the responsibility to keep a true record of our adventure in Egypt. Within those pages, and those pages alone, can Hamid Reza's terrible secret be told."

Dear Diary,

Well, here I sit under my very own oak tree once again. I came home from Egypt two days ago and already it seems like a million years! Was I *really* there, or did I just dream it all? Actually, I know it wasn't a dream because I still have the mosquito bites to prove it! Pete and I counted our bites to see who had the most and he won. He had 53 and I only had 42!

I'd give anything to be back on that boat sailing the Nile. It was so beautiful and peaceful; I'll never forget it. When I told Beth, she was *so* jealous I think she could have strangled me!

It's hard to believe now that all those things really happened.

Mom nearly fainted when she found out Dad had almost been captured by terrorists. To think that Mr. Reza could actually have tried to betray a friend for money! It's terrible! But Dad says each one of us is capable of doing something like that—or even worse. I wonder what I would have done if I were in Mr. Reza's shoes and were as scared and worried as he was?

I guess the most important thing is that he was sorry. God forgave him and so did my Dad. Now he'll try to do better.

I've learned something, too, I think! Yes, Mr. Oak Tree, I'm an older, (wiser??) person since I got back from Egypt. At least, I hope so!